Uninvited Ghosts

Penelope Lively

Uninvited Ghosts
and Other Stories

Illustrated by
John Lawrence

E. P. DUTTON   NEW YORK

Library of Congress Cataloging in Publication Data

Lively, Penelope.
  Uninvited ghosts and other stories.

  Contents: A Martian comes to stay—The disastrous
dog—Uninvited ghosts—[etc.]
  1. Children's stories, English. [1. Fantasy.
2. Short stories] I. Lawrence, John, date ill.
II. Title.
PZ7.L7397Un 1985 [Fic] 84-26035
ISBN 0-525-44165-4

The title story, "Uninvited Ghosts," was first published in *Frank and Polly Muir's Big Dipper* (Heinemann 1981). "Princess by Mistake" appeared in *Jubilee Jackanory*, published by the BBC in 1977, and "Dragon Tunnel" in *Allsorts 6*, edited by Ann Thwaite and published by Methuen Children's Books in 1974.

Contents

A Martian Comes to Stay

It was on the second day of Peter's holiday with his grandmother that the Martian came to the cottage. There was a knock at the door and when he went to open it there was this small green person with webbed feet and eyes on the end of stumpy antennae who said, perfectly politely, "I wonder if I might bother you for the loan of a spanner?"

"Sure," said Peter. "I'll ask my gran."

Gran was in the back garden, it being a nice sunny day. Peter said, "There's a Martian at the door who'd like to borrow a spanner."

Gran looked at him over her knitting. "Is there, dear? Have a look in grandad's toolbox, there should be one there."

That's not what your grandmother would have said? No, nor mine either but Peter's gran was an unusual lady, as you will discover. Grandad had died a few years earlier and she lived alone in this isolated cottage in the country, growing vegetables and keeping chickens, and Peter liked going to stay with her more than almost anything he could think of. Gran was not like most people. She was unflappable and what you might call open-minded, which accounts for everything that happened next.

Peter found the spanner and took it back to the Martian, who held out a rather oddly constructed hand and thanked him warmly. "We've got some trouble with the gears or something and had to make an emergency landing. And now the mechanic says he left his tools back at base. I ask you! It's all a mystery to me—I'm just the steward. Anyway—thanks a lot. I'll bring it back in a minute." And he padded away up the lane. There was no one around, but then there wasn't likely to be: the cottage was a quarter of a mile from the village and hardly anyone came by except the occasional farm tractor and the odd holidaymaker who'd got lost. Peter went back into the garden.

"Should have offered him a cup of tea," said Gran. "He'll have had a fair journey, I shouldn't wonder."

"Yes," said Peter. "I didn't think of that."

In precisely three minutes time there was a knock at the door. The Martian was there, looking distinctly agitated. He said, "They've gone."

"Who's gone?" said Peter.

"The others. The spaceship. All of them. They've taken off and left me."

Gran, by now, had come through from the garden. She hitched her specs up her nose and looked down at the Martian, who was about three and a half feet high. "You'd best come in," she said, "while we have a think. Gone, you say? Where was it, this thing of yours?"

"Over there," said the Martian, pointing across the lane.

"Ah," said Gran. "Ted Thomas's field."

"The one with the bullocks in," added Peter.

"Bullocks?" said the Martian.

"Big brown animals," explained Peter.

"Animals?" said the Martian.

"Creatures that walk about and eat, like you and me, only different."

The Martian nodded. "I saw them, then. I hoped they were harmless."

"They are," said Peter.

"But curious," said Gran. "They'd have wanted to have a look at this space whatsit, wouldn't they? Stand round it in a circle, making heavy breathing noises. Would they be a bit jumpy, your friends, Mr er . . . ?"

11

"Very," said the Martian. "We tend to be, when we get off-course. I'm dead jumpy right now. For one thing, I'm frightened of that thing in the corner that makes a ticking noise. Is it going to blow up?"

Peter explained about clocks.

Gran, meanwhile, had put the kettle on. "The way I see it, these friends of Mr, er . . . looked out and saw Ted's bullocks and lost their heads, and who's to blame them? Still, it's not very nice, leaving him stuck here like this. I mean, it's not as though we can give the village taxi a ring and get him home like that. I don't know what's to be done for the best, I really don't. Meanwhile, we'll have a nice cup of tea."

Tea and a couple of digestive biscuits cheered the Martian up. He sat on the footstool by the stove and apologised for being such a nuisance. "Not at all," said Gran. "We don't get a lot of company round here. It's you I'm bothered about. But anyway, we've got the attic room empty so you're welcome to stop until we can work something out. You'll be company for Peter." She gazed for a moment at the visitor and went on, delicately, "Are you, er, young or old, as you might say?"

"I'm three hundred and twenty-seven," said the Martian.

"Ah," said Gran. "Then there's a bit of an age-gap, on the face of it. Peter's nine. Still, it's the spirit that counts, isn't it? That's what I always find, anyway."

The Martian was an adaptable visitor. He felt the cold rather and preferred to sit right up against the stove and once, with further apologies, got into the oven for a bit to warm up. "Get a lot of sun, do you, where you come from?" asked Gran. But the Martian was rather vague about his home surroundings; it was different, he said—adding hastily that of course he didn't mean it was better. Once or twice he looked out of the window a trifle nervously. He wanted to know why the trees kept moving.

"It's the wind, dear," said Gran, who tended to take people into the family once she liked them.

"They're not aggressive?"

"Not to speak of."

Later, they watched television. The Martian was interested but inclined to raise questions. "Is it true to life?" he enquired, in the middle of 'Top of the Pops.'

"No," said Peter. "At least not most people's."

"What about this?" asked the Martian presently, when 'Dallas' was on.

"I wouldn't say so," said Gran. "But then I've had a limited experience."

He appreciated 'Zoo Quest,' which was about South American creatures. "That's Nature," said Gran. "It's very highly thought of nowadays. Time I got us something to eat." She looked doubtfully at the Martian. "You're not on a special diet or anything like that, I hope?"

But the Martian proved admirably easy to feed. He was a bit wary of sausages but discovered a passion for jam tarts. "You tuck in," said Gran. "You'll be hungry, after that journey."

Over the next couple of days he settled in nicely. He insisted on helping with the washing-up and played Monopoly with Peter. Peter won every time, which he found embarrassing. The Martian didn't seem to grasp the idea of making money. "I'm sorry," he said apologetically. "Why do I want to have more and more of these bits of paper?"

"So that you can buy things," Peter explained.

"Things to eat?"

14

"Well, no. It's streets and hotels and things, in the game."

"Mind," said Gran, "he's got a point. It's something I've wondered about myself. Maybe you should try a game of cards."

They played Snap and Rummy but this wasn't much better. The Martian preferred not to win.

"To my mind," said Gran, "they've got a different outlook on life, wherever he comes from." She was knitting the Martian a sweater now. "Would you come here a minute, dear, just so I can measure it across the chest." The Martian stood in front of her obligingly.

Gran stretched the knitting across his greenish, rather leathery body. "It's to keep the chill out," she went on. "Being as you feel the cold so. I've no objection at all to a person going around in the altogether if that's what they're used to, let's get that clear. There—that's a nice fit."

The Martian was quite embarrassingly grateful.

He did not venture outside, which seemed on the whole advisable in any case. Neighbours, in remote country districts, tend to be inquisitive about other people's visitors and the Martian would be an odd one to have to explain. "I suppose," said Peter, "we could say he's a distant relative who's come from somewhere abroad."

"That's not going to satisfy some folks I could name," said Gran. "Not with him being as unusual-looking as he is. Even if we said he took after another branch of the family. No, it's best if he stays put till his friends come back. D'you think they'll take long, dear?"

The Martian shook his head doubtfully. He said he thought they would come, eventually, but that they might be having difficulty finding the right spot again. "Well, not to worry," said Gran. "We'll just bide our time till they do."

After several days the Martian overcame his worries about trees and various noises that bothered him such as birds and dogs barking, and sat in a deckchair in the garden, wearing Gran's sweater and with a rug round him. On one of these occasions old Mr Briggs from down the lane came past with his dog and stopped for a moment to chat to Gran over the wall. "Ah," he said, glancing over her shoulder. "Got another of your grandchildren stopping with you, then?"

"In a manner of speaking," said Gran evasively.

Mr Briggs departed, calling over his shoulder, "See you at the village fête, Saturday."

Gran sat down again. "It's a shame we can't take him along to the fête. Be ever so interesting for him. I mean, it's what you want, when you're in foreign parts—have a look at how other people set about things. The Flower Show'll be a treat this year, with the good weather we've been having."

The Martian said wistfully that he'd love to go.

"I wonder," said Gran. "Let's see now. S'pose we . . ."

And then Peter had a brilliant idea. In the cupboard under the stairs there was an old push-chair that had been used for him and his sister when they were small. If they put the Martian in that and covered him up with a pram-rug and put something round his head, he could pass for a small child. Gran clapped her hands. "Clever boy! There now, we'll have ourselves an outing!" The Martian beamed, if someone with an-tennae, a mouth somewhat like a letter-box and not much else by way of features can be said to beam.

17

"You know," Gran confided to Peter later on, when they were alone, "I've really took to him. You can tell he's been brought up nicely, from his manners. There's some human beings I know would be put to shame."

The day of the fête was fine and dry. The Martian was installed in the push-chair, swathed in a blue rug that Gran had crocheted a long time ago and with an old pixie hood that had belonged to Peter's sister on his head. His antennae poked out through two holes, which did not look quite right, so they had to fix a sunshade to the handles of the push-chair and drape some muslin over this; in this way the Martian was only dimly visible as a muffled form. "We'll say he's sensitive to sunstroke," said Gran, "if anyone gets nosy." They set off for the village with Peter in charge of the push-chair.

The Martian was fascinated with everything he saw. He asked them to stop for him to admire the Amoco Garage with its swags of flapping plastic flags and brightly coloured signs about Four Star Petrol and Credit Cards Accepted. He found it, he declared, very beautiful.

"Well," said Gran doubtfully, "to my mind that's on the garish side, but I suppose it's a matter of taste." The Martian said humbly that he probably hadn't been here long enough yet to be much of a judge of these things. He gazed at the display of baked beans tins and cornflakes packets in the window of the Minimarket and asked anxiously if that would be considered handsome. "Not really," said Peter. "I mean, it's the sort of thing that's so ordinary you don't really notice."

"He's seeing a different angle to us," said Gran. "Stands to reason, when you think about it."

The smell of petrol made him sneeze. Mrs Lilly from the Post Office, who happened to be passing at the time, craned her head round to stare into the pushchair. "Bless its little heart, then! Tishoo!" She bent down. "Little boy or a little girl, is it?"

"Boy," said Gran. "I wouldn't be surprised if that cold wasn't giving way to something worse," she added loudly. Mrs Lilly backed away.

They reached the village green, on which the fête was taking place. The band was already playing. The Martian peered out from under the sunshade. "Watch it!" said Peter warningly. "People'll see you." The Martian apologised. "It's just that it's all so exciting."

"We always put on a good show," said Gran modestly. "It's a question of upstaging Great Snoggington down the road, up to a point," she explained. The Martian, under the sunshade, nodded. Gran pointed out the Vicar and the head teacher from the village school and Mr Soper who ran the pub. "They are your leaders?" asked the Martian.

"In a manner of speaking," said Gran.

They toured the Bring and Buy stall and the Flower Tent. Gran paused to cast a professional eye over the

19

sweet peas. Peter took out his money to see if he had
enough left for another ice cream. Neither of them
saw Susie Stubbs, who was aged three and in Peter's
opinion the most appalling brat in the village, sidle up
to the push-chair. She put out a fat finger and poked
the Martian, who sat perfectly still. Susie stuck her face
under the sunshade.

There was an earsplitting shriek. Susie's mum, busy
in the middle of a piece of juicy gossip with a friend,
broke off and came rushing over.

"Ooooh . . . !" wailed Susie. "An 'orrible fing! An
'orrible fing like a snail! Oooh—I don' like it! Want to
go home! Want my mum! Take it away! Ooh, an
'orrible fing in that pram!"

"There, my pet," cooed Susie's mum. "There,
there . . . Did she have a nasty fright, then? Let's buy
her an iced lolly, shall we?"

"'Orrible fing . . ." howled Susie, pointing at the push-chair.

Gran glared. She jerked the push-chair away, nearly dislodging the Martian.

"There now, my duckie," said Susie's mum. "Why don't you ask the little girl if she'd like to come and play, then?"

"Boy," snapped Gran. "Pity he's got such a shocking case of chicken-pox or he'd have liked to, wouldn't you then, Johnnie? 'Bye now, Mrs Stubbs."

An interested group of observers had gathered. Peter and Gran departed hastily. "Sorry about that," said Gran to the Martian. The Martian replied politely that where he came from also young people were sometimes inclined to be tiresome.

They left the Flower Tent, pausing for Gran to have a word with one or two friends. Curiosity, though, had now been aroused; people kept casting interested glances at the push-chair. "That your Ron's youngest?" enquired Mrs Binns from the shop. "Eh?" said Gran loudly; she was expert at producing sudden onsets of deafness when convenient.

Outside, they sat down to watch the police dog display. One of the dogs, which was supposed to be tracking a man who was supposed to be an escaped criminal, kept rushing over and sniffing at the push-chair. "Get away, you brute," snarled Gran. The Martian, beneath the sunshade, kept bravely silent but had turned quite pale when Peter took a look at him. He fetched some orange juice from the Refreshment Tent. "Thank you," said the Martian faintly.

A stout figure swathed in several Indian bedspreads sat under a sign which declared her to be MADAME RITA, THE INTERNATIONALLY FAMOUS PALMIST AND FORTUNE TELLER. "That's the Vicar's wife," said Gran. "I'm not having her nosing around my future." Nevertheless, she veered in that direction. The Vicar's wife, her face blotted out by an enormous pair of sunglasses, seized Gran's hand and predicted a tall dark stranger next Thursday. "That'll be him that comes to read the meter," said Gran. "Well-built, I'd call him, rather than tall, but never mind."

The Vicar's wife, bending down, lifted the muslin draped over the Martian's sunshade. "What about the baby, then—let's have your hand, duckie." She gave

a gasp of horror. "Oh, my goodness, the poor little dear, whatever . . ."

"Whatever what?" said Gran frostily.

The Vicar's wife dropped the muslin. "Well, he's a nice little thing, of course, but . . . well . . . unusual."

Gran gave her a withering look. "I'd say those specs you've got on aren't doing you any good, Mrs Mervyn. Fashionable they may be but not what I'd call service-able. Well, I'd best be getting on."

"Whew!" said Peter, when they were out of earshot. "It's getting a bit dodgy here."

Gran agreed. "Anyway, he's seen a bit of our way of life, that's the main thing. We'll get home now."

But the damage had been done. There was gossip. The village had been alerted. The next day, three people turned up at the cottage declaring that they happened to be passing and hadn't seen Gran for a month of Sundays and had been wondering how she was. Gran managed to get rid of them all. The Martian sat by the stove saying sadly that he was afraid he was becoming a problem. "It's not you that's the problem," said Gran. "It's human nature."

All the same, they realised that he could not stay there for ever. "At least not without us becoming world famous," said Peter. "And him being put on the telly and that kind of thing."

"I shouldn't care for that," said the Martian in alarm. "I'm basically very shy."

They discussed what was to be done. The Martian said he thought that probably his companions would be trying to find the spot at which they had landed but were having navigational problems.

"Anything you can think of we could do to lend a hand?" enquired Gran.

"We could signal," said Peter. "In their language. He could tell us what to say."

The Martian became quite excited. He'd need some kind of radio transmitter, he said.

Gran shook her head. "I've not got one of those to hand. But there's Jim's big torch up in the attic. We could flash that, like, when it's dark."

They had their first signal session that evening. The Martian dictated a series of long and short flashes and Peter and Gran took it in turns to stand at the window with the lights off, waving the torch at the sky. Gran thoroughly enjoyed it. She wanted to put in all sorts of extras like invitations to tea and enquiries about whether they preferred fruit cake or a nice jam sponge. She hoped there wouldn't be misunderstandings. "We don't want one of them satellites coming down in Ted Thomas's field. Or a bunch of them R.A.F. blokes."

But nothing happened. They decided to try again the next night.

They had been at it for an hour or two—with a break to watch 'Coronation Street,' to which the Martian was becoming dangerously addicted—when there was a knock at the door.

"Oh, it's you, Bert," said Gran. "What's up, then? Don't you start telling me I've got no telly licence, because I have. Top drawer of the dresser, have a look for yourself."

The village policeman was standing there. He said heavily, "I'm obliged to ask you if I might come in and look round the premises, Mrs Tranter."

"What's all this posh talk for?" said Gran. "Come on in. Help yourself." She put the torch on the table.

The policeman eyed it. "Would you mind telling me what you've been employing that for the use of, Mrs Tranter?"

"That," snapped Gran, "is a torch, and if you don't know what torches are for, Bert Davies, then you'll never make sergeant, frankly."

The policeman, a little red now around the neck, met Gran's glare valiantly, eyeball to eyeball. "Would you by any chance, Mrs Tranter, have been passing information to a foreign power?"

There was an awful silence. Peter and the Martian, who was cowering behind the stove, exchanged nervous glances.

"Bert Davies," said Gran at last, "I've known you since you was in nappies. You come here asking that kind of thing once more—just once more—and I'm off down the village to have a word with your mum." She glared at the policeman, who was now a rich strawberry colour to the roots of his hair, and was backing towards the door.

"There's been reports," he said. "Reports about flashing lights and that. It's my duty to investigate."

"It's your duty to get back to the village and see about them motor bike boys that's always charging through over the speed limit," snapped Gran.

It was at that moment that Peter heard a curious whirring noise from somewhere outside. The policeman, mercifully, was too unnerved to pay any attention, if indeed he had heard anything; he retreated to his car, with as much dignity as he could manage, and drove off into the night . . .

. . . At precisely the same time as something brightly spiced with lights loomed above Ted Thomas's field, hovered for a moment, and sank below the line of the hedge.

Peter cried, "They're here!"

"And none before time too," said Gran. The Martian was already on his feet and hurrying to the door. He paused, trying to take off his sweater. "You keep that," said Gran. "Someone might like to copy the pattern, up where you come from."

The Martian held out his hand. "Thank you very much for having me. I've enjoyed it enormously. I wish I could suggest . . ." He hesitated.

"No, dear," said Gran. "Return visits are out, I'm afraid. Foreign travel doesn't appeal to me nowadays. A week in Llandudno in August does me nicely."

From the field, there was still that whirring noise, and a shimmering orange glow. "Better go," said Peter anxiously, "before anyone comes."

The Martian nodded. He padded out and down the lane. They saw him get smaller and more indistinct and turn in at the gate into the field and then the orange glow got larger and the whirring louder and there was a snap of bright lights and a rush and then silence and darkness.

Gran closed the door. "That, I take it," she said, "was one of them flying saucers. Pity we couldn't have taken a picture. It would have been nice for my album.

Put the torch back in the attic, would you, dear. And put that spanner back in your grandad's toolbox, while you're at it. Good thing we had that by us, or we'd never have been able to lend a hand in the first place. I should have made him up some sandwiches for the journey, you know."

And she settled down by the stove with her knitting.

The Disastrous Dog

Some people buy dogs. Some people are given dogs. Some people are taken over by dogs, as you might say. I'll tell you what happened to the Ropers, just in case *your* parents ever decide to get a dog from the local Animal Sanctuary.

Mr Roper was in favour of getting a dog from the Sanctuary because he didn't see the point of paying good money for something when you can get it free. Mrs Roper thought it would be nice to give a home to a poor unwanted dog. Paul, who was nine, didn't really care where the dog came from so long as they had one.

He'd been wanting a dog for ages, and now that they'd moved to a house down the end of a long lane, with no neighbours, outside the village, his father had come round to the idea. A guard dog, it was to be, a sensible efficient anti-burglar useful kind of dog.

The Animal Sanctuary seethed with dogs, in all shapes and sizes. They rushed around in wire netting enclosures, all barking at once, tail-wagging, jumping up and down. The Warden pointed out several promising creatures: a brown spaniel, all ears and paws, an elegant collie, a rather raffish mongrel with a penetrating bark. Mr and Mrs Roper moved along the fence, inspecting. Mrs Roper, who was a pushover for both animals and children, patted and cooed and allowed herself to be licked. Paul struck up a friendship with an over-excited yellow puppy.

"Oy . . . !" Paul looked around.

"Oy! You there . . ."

His parents were on the far side of the yard, discussing a terrier. The Warden had gone. The voice came from none of them. And I must explain that it was, and Paul immediately understood this, no ordinary voice. It was, as it were, a voice in the head—person to person, invisible, like a telephone. But the words that were said were ordinary and straightforward. Standard English. And so was the tone, which was distinctly bossy.

He looked at the dogs, carefully. They were all dashing around except for one, a nondescript brown animal with a stumpy tail and one white ear, which stood squarely beside the fence staring at Paul.

Paul glanced over at his parents; they were not looking in his direction. He stared back at the brown dog. "Did you say something?" he asked, feeling foolish.

"Too right I did," said the dog. "Do you live in a house or a flat?"

"A house. In the country."

"Central heating? Garden?"

"Yes. Listen, how come you . . ."

The dog interrupted. "Sounds a reasonable billet. Get your parents over here and I'll do my stuff. Homeless dog act. Never fails."

"Can they all?" asked Paul, waving at the other dogs. "Talk?"

The dog spluttered contemptuously. " 'Course not. Ordinary mob, that's all they are."

There was something not altogether attractive about the dog's personality, but Paul could not help being intrigued. "Then how did you learn?"

"Because I know what's what," snapped the dog.

"And why me? Why don't you talk to my dad?"

"Unfortunately," said the dog, "the adult of the species tends to have what you might call a closed mind. I've tried, believe you me. No go. It's only you small fry that are at all receptive. More's the pity. Go on—tell your mum and dad to come over and have a look at me."

Paul wasn't entirely pleased at being called small fry. He hesitated. The dog came closer to the fence and stared up at him, with slightly narrowed eyes. "Think about it," he said. "We could set up in the entertainment business. There'd be something in it for you—plenty of perks. The Dog That Can Count. The Dog That Can Read Your Thoughts. We could be on the telly. The sky's the limit."

"We just want a dog that can bark," said Paul.

The dog flung back his head and let out a volley of ear-splitting barks. "That do?"

Mr and Mrs Roper, abandoning the terrier, had come across. The dog immediately hurled himself at the wire fence with a devastating display of tail-wagging, grinning and licking. When Mrs Roper stooped to pat him he rolled over on his back with his eyes shut and squirmed in apparent ecstasy. Mrs Roper said, "Oh, isn't he sweet!" The dog, briefly, opened one eye. He then got up and squatted in front of Mr Roper in an attitude of abject obedience. Finally, he rushed off as though in pursuit of an unseen enemy and did some more barking, of hideous ferocity and quite deafening.

Well, I don't need to tell you what happened.

To say that the dog settled in is to put it mildly: he established himself. Within a matter of days. He got his basket moved from the cloakroom by feigning illness; Mrs Roper, gazing down at him, said anxiously,

"I think perhaps he's cold in here. We'd better let him sleep in the kitchen by the boiler." The dog feebly wagged his tail and staggered to his feet. The first time they took him for a walk he developed a limp after the first mile. Paul examined his paws. He said, "I can't see anything wrong."

"Shut up," snarled the dog. "I'm crippled. I'm not one for all this hearty outdoor stuff, let's get that straight from the start."

Paul had to carry him home.

On the fourth day the dog said, "Tell her I don't like that rabbit-flavoured meat she's giving me. I want the beef and oxtail flavour. And more biscuits."

"Tell her yourself," said Paul sulkily. He was getting tired of being ordered about.

"Some people," snapped the dog, "might find

things going a bit awkward, if they don't look out and act obliging. Some people might find for instance that their mother's best vase would get knocked off the table and broken and *then* who'd get the blame? Some people might find that things mysteriously disappeared, like their dad's pipe and people's gloves, and *then* who'd be nagged at to get down and find them?"

"You wouldn't!" said Paul, without conviction.

"Try me," said the dog.

"Why's she to believe I know what you like and what you don't like?"

"Children have a special relationship with animals," said the dog. "It's a well-known fact."

They called him Mick. It didn't seem to suit him particularly, but then it would have been hard to know what would. "What's your name?" Paul had asked, on the first day.

"Depends," said the dog. "One has run through a good many, as it happens. Suit yourselves."

So Mick it was.

His favourite activity was sleeping. Preferably after a hefty meal and on the best sofa or one of the beds. "Most dogs," said Paul, "rush about all day sniffing at things and asking to be taken for walks."

Mick yawned. "That's their problem. Me, I've learned how to keep my head down and have a comfortable life. Push off, there's a good boy, I want a kip."

To begin with, he barked at the postman and the milkman and the man who came to read the meter. On the fifth day, he slept through the window–cleaner and a man selling brushes and a lady collecting for the Red Cross. Paul said, "You're supposed to bark. That's what they got you for."

"I barked my head off all yesterday," said Mick sullenly. "Besides, there's a rate for the job. If they want more action, then what about something extra on the side? The odd chocolate biscuit. A nice chop."

Mr Roper, by now, was beginning to have doubts. He observed that Mick seemed a somewhat slothful sort of dog. Mrs Roper, always keen to see the best in people, wondered if perhaps he was a rather old dog and too much shouldn't be expected. Mick, looking worn, limped to his food bowl and stood there gazing at her soulfully.

Mr Roper said he was to be put out in the garden for part of every day, and no nonsense. Mick sat on the front doorstep, glowering. When visitors arrived for Sunday lunch he hurled himself at them, barking hysterically, and tore a strip out of Uncle Harry's trousers. The smallest cousin burst into tears and refused to get out of the car and Mick was shut in the garage. When he was let out he was in a towering rage. "You're supposed to be able to tell the difference between friends and possible burglars," said Paul. "That was my uncle. Mum had to spend all afternoon apologising."

"They said do guard dog stuff," snarled Mick, "so I did guard dog stuff. Anyway I didn't care for the fellow."

Other people, Paul realised, with resignation, have engaging roly-poly puppies; other people have dear old faithful sheepdogs; other people have sprightly interesting terriers. They had Mick. It was rather like having a very demanding guest in the house who is never going to leave. Only Paul, of course, knew exactly what sort of a person—dog—he was, but even his parents were beginning to be a little resentful.

"He is awfully greedy," said Mrs Roper. "I don't know how it's happened but he's somehow got me giving him *three* meals a day now." Paul knew only too well how it had happened. "He's lazy," said Mr Roper. "No two ways about it, I'm afraid." He took Mick for a five mile walk; Mick rolled in a muddy ditch and then came back and rolled on the sitting room carpet. "That'll teach 'em," he said. Paul, looking at his mother's face, realised with interest that Mick might go too far before long.

"I thought," he said, "we were going into the entertainment business. Do tricks. Go on the telly."

Mick, sprawled on the sofa, opened one eye. "Tricks? You must be joking, mate. That's work, that is. I know when I'm well off."

He got fatter and fatter. His attacks on the postman were more and more unconvincing. But the crunch came on the day the men came to collect the television for repair when everyone was out. They went round to the back door, which had been left unlocked, came in, removed the television and drove away in a van.

Mrs Roper, when they brought it back, apologised. "I'm afraid our dog must have been a bit of a nuisance. I'd meant to lock him up before you came."

The television man laughed. "Not him. Fast asleep, he was, and then woke up and took one look and scarpered outside. Wouldn't say boo to a goose, he wouldn't."

That did it. "He's useless," said Mr Roper. Mrs Roper, always prepared to give the benefit of the doubt, suggested that perhaps Mick knew the difference between television repair men and burglars. "Not unless he could read the writing on the side of the van," said Mr Roper grimly. "He's going back to the Animal Sanctuary, and that's that."

Paul, secretly, heaved a sigh of relief. Mick had gone too far. And now, with any luck, they could get another dog: a speechless dog-like dog. What would happen to Mick he could not imagine, but he had a fairly strong feeling that he was well able to take care of himself. He said to him, "Why didn't you bite them? I mean, there they were, walking off with the telly . . ."

"I wasn't going to start mixing it with blokes like that," said Mick shortly. "I didn't like the look in their eye. Could have done me a nasty injury. I know when to keep a low profile, I do."

"They're going to take you back to the Animal Sanctuary."

Mick looked supercilious. "No skin off my nose. To

tell the truth, I've known cushier billets than this. I'll tell you what I've got my eye on for next time—nice old lady. Soft touch, old ladies can be, I've tried 'em before. Plenty of nosh and no nonsense about exercise. I'll be all right—you see."

And something tells me that he was. But if ever you go to get a dog from an Animal Sanctuary, and happen to run across a brown mongrel with one white ear— well, I should think very carefully . . .

Uninvited Ghosts

Marian and Simon were sent to bed early on the day that the Brown family moved house. By then everyone had lost their temper with everyone else; the cat had been sick on the sitting-room carpet; the dog had run away twice. If you have ever moved you will know what kind of a day it had been. Packing cases and newspaper all over the place . . . sandwiches instead of proper meals . . . the kettle lost and a wardrobe stuck on the stairs and Mrs Brown's favourite vase broken. There was bread and baked beans for supper, the television wouldn't work and the water wasn't hot so when all was said and done the children didn't object too violently to being packed off to bed. They'd had enough, too. They had one last argument about who was going to sleep by the window, put on their pyjamas, got into bed, switched the lights out . . . and it was at that point that the ghost came out of the bottom drawer of the chest of drawers.

It oozed out, a grey cloudy shape about three feet long smelling faintly of woodsmoke, sat down on a chair and began to hum to itself. It looked like a bundle of bedclothes, except that it was not solid: you could see, quite clearly, the cushion on the chair beneath it.

Marian gave a shriek. "That's a ghost!"

"Oh, be quiet, dear, do," said the ghost. "That noise goes right through my head. And it's not nice to call people names." It took out a ball of wool and some needles and began to knit.

What would you have done? Well, yes—Simon and Marian did just that and I daresay you can imagine what happened. You try telling your mother that you can't get to sleep because there's a ghost sitting in the room clacking its knitting-needles and humming. Mrs Brown said the kind of things she could be expected to say and the ghost continued sitting there knitting and humming and Mrs Brown went out, banging the door and saying threatening things about if there's so much as another word from either of you . . . .

"She can't see it," said Marian to Simon.

" 'Course not, dear," said the ghost. "It's the kiddies I'm here for. Love kiddies, I do. We're going to be ever such friends."

"Go away!" yelled Simon. "This is our house now!"

"No it isn't," said the ghost smugly. "Always been here, I have. A hundred years and more. Seen plenty of families come and go, I have. Go to bye-byes now, there's good children."

The children glared at it and buried themselves under the bedclothes. And, eventually, slept.

The next night it was there again. This time it was smoking a long white pipe and reading a newspaper dated 1842. Beside it was a second grey cloudy shape. "Hello, dearies," said the ghost. "Say how do you do to my Auntie Edna."

"She can't come here too," wailed Marian.

"Oh yes she can," said the ghost. "Always comes here in August, does Auntie. She likes a change."

Auntie Edna was even worse, if possible. She sucked peppermint drops that smelled so strong that Mrs Brown, when she came to kiss the children good night, looked suspiciously under their pillows. She also sang hymns in a loud squeaky voice. The children lay there groaning and the ghosts sang and rustled the news-papers and ate peppermints.

The next night there were three of them. "Meet Uncle Charlie!" said the first ghost. The children groaned.

"And Jip," said the ghost. "Here, Jip, good dog—come and say hello to the kiddies, then." A large grey dog that you could see straight through came out from under the bed, wagging its tail. The cat, who had been curled up beside Marian's feet (it was supposed to sleep in the kitchen, but there are always ways for a resourceful cat to get what it wants), gave a howl and shot on

top of the wardrobe, where it sat spitting. The dog lay down in the middle of the rug and set about scratching itself vigorously; evidently it had ghost fleas, too.

Uncle Charlie was unbearable. He had a loud cough that kept going off like a machine-gun and he told the longest most pointless stories the children had ever heard. He said he too loved kiddies and he knew kiddies loved stories. In the middle of the seventh story the children went to sleep out of sheer boredom.

The following week the ghosts left the bedroom and were to be found all over the house. The children had no peace at all. They'd be quietly doing their home-work and all of a sudden Auntie Edna would be breathing down their necks reciting arithmetic tables. The original ghost took to sitting on top of the tele-vision with his legs in front of the picture. Uncle Charlie told his stories all through the best programmes and the dog lay permanently at the top of the stairs. The Browns' cat became quite hysterical, refused to eat and went to live on the top shelf of the kitchen dresser.

Something had to be done. Marian and Simon also were beginning to show the effects; their mother decided they looked peaky and bought an appalling sticky brown vitamin medicine from the chemists to strengthen them. "It's the ghosts!" wailed the children. "We don't need vitamins!" Their mother said severely that she didn't want to hear another word of this silly nonsense about ghosts. Auntie Edna, who was sitting smirking on the other side of the kitchen table at that very moment, nodded vigorously and took out a packet of humbugs which she sucked noisily.

"We've got to get them to go and live somewhere else," said Marian. But where, that was the problem, and how? It was then that they had a bright idea. On Sunday the Browns were all going to see their uncle who was rather rich and lived alone in a big house with thick carpets everywhere and empty rooms and the biggest colour television you ever saw. Plenty of room for ghosts.

They were very cunning. They suggested to the ghosts that they might like a drive in the country. The ghosts said at first that they were quite comfortable where they were, thank you, and they didn't fancy these new-fangled motor-cars, not at their time of life. But then Auntie Edna remembered that she liked looking at the pretty flowers and the trees and finally they agreed to give it a try. They sat in a row on the back shelf of the car. Mrs Brown kept asking why there was such a strong smell of peppermint and Mr Brown kept roaring at Simon and Marian to keep still while he was driving. The fact was that the ghosts were shoving them; it was like being nudged by three cold damp flannels. And the ghost dog, who had come along too of course, was car-sick.

When they got to Uncle Dick's the ghosts came in

and had a look round. They liked the expensive carpets and the enormous television. They slid in and out of the wardrobes and walked through the doors and the walls and sent Uncle Dick's budgerigars into a decline from which they have never recovered. Nice place, they said, nice and comfy.

"Why not stay here?" said Simon, in an offhand tone.

"Couldn't do that," said the ghosts firmly. "No kiddies. Dull. We like a place with a bit of life to it." And they piled back into the car and sang hymns all the way home to the Browns' house. They also ate toast. There were real toast-crumbs on the floor and the children got the blame.

Simon and Marian were in despair. The ruder they were to the ghosts the more the ghosts liked it. "Cheeky!" they said indulgently. "What a cheeky little pair of kiddies! There now . . . come and give uncle a kiss." The children weren't even safe in the bath. One or other of the ghosts would come and sit on the taps and talk to them. Uncle Charlie had produced a mouth organ and played the same tune over and over again; it was quite excruciating. The children went around with their hands over their ears. Mrs Brown took them to the doctor to find out if there was something wrong with their hearing. The children knew better than to say anything to the doctor about the ghosts. It was pointless saying anything to anyone.

I don't know what would have happened if Mrs Brown hadn't happened to make friends with Mrs Walker from down the road. Mrs Walker had twin babies, and one day she brought the babies along for tea.

Now one baby is bad enough. Two babies are trouble in a big way. These babies created pandemonium. When they weren't both howling they were crawling around the floor pulling the tablecloths off the tables or hitting their heads on the chairs and hauling the books out of the bookcases. They threw their food all over the kitchen and flung cups of milk on the floor. Their mother mopped up after them and every time she tried to have a conversation with Mrs Brown the babies bawled in chorus so that no one could hear a word.

In the middle of this the ghosts appeared. One baby was yelling its head off and the other was glueing pieces of chewed up bread onto the front of the television. The ghosts swooped down on them with happy cries. "Oh!" they trilled. "Bless their little hearts then, diddums, give auntie a smile then." And the babies stopped in mid-howl and gazed at the ghosts. The ghosts cooed at the babies and the babies cooed at the ghosts. The ghosts chattered to the babies and sang them songs and the babies chattered back and were as good as gold for the next hour and their mother had the first proper conversation she'd had in weeks. When

they went the ghosts stood in a row at the window, waving.

Simon and Marian knew when to seize an opportunity. That evening they had a talk with the ghosts. At first the ghosts raised objections. They didn't fancy the idea of moving, they said; you got set in your ways, at their age; Auntie Edna reckoned a strange house would be the death of her.

The children talked about the babies, relentlessly.

And the next day they led the ghosts down the road, followed by the ghost dog, and into the Walkers' house. Mrs Walker doesn't know to this day why the babies, who had been screaming for the last half hour, suddenly stopped and broke into great smiles. And she has never understood why, from that day forth, the babies became the most tranquil, quiet, amiable babies in the area. The ghosts kept the babies amused from morning to night. The babies thrived; the ghosts were happy; the ghost dog, who was actually a bitch, settled down so well that she had puppies which is one of the most surprising aspects of the whole business. The Brown children heaved a sigh of relief and got back to normal life. The babies, though, I have to tell you, grew up somewhat peculiar.

The Dragon Tunnel

Dragons . . . Do you ever think about dragons? I daresay you don't, and if you do I've no doubt you reckon they're fairy-story stuff, along with goblins and princesses and all that. Right? You'd laugh if someone came along and span you a story about there once being real-life dragons walking around Oxfordshire or Berkshire or Middlesex, wouldn't you? Go on, you'd say, pull the other one, it's got bells on . . . Well, that's as may be, but all the same I'd like you to listen to something I can tell you, and you can make up your own mind what you think about it. I'll just mention, though, in passing, that I'm not a fanciful sort of a bloke. Down-to-earth, that's me. Bill Chaundy's my name, and I run the pub here in Ledsham. And I'm not telling you how I know the story, except that it happened thirty years ago or so, when I was a boy. As I say, you can take it or leave it.

The church in the village here has paintings on the walls—very old paintings, hard to see unless you know they're there. Quite famous, though, they are—people come miles to see them, who've a taste for that kind of thing. There's one painting of the Day of Judgement, with scarlet devils shovelling the wicked into hell and the luckier lot scrambling up a ladder to heaven. And then there's a picture of a dragon chasing some people around some fields—dead scared they look, too. The fields have willows round the edge, and a river winding through them, and as a matter of fact they look just like the willows and the river that are around the village today. There's a booklet in the church that tells you about the paintings. The dragon one, it says, illustrates an ancient local tradition of a dragon that lived under the village and emerged from time to time to ravage the countryside. The booklet doesn't approve of that kind of thing—stories about dragons and that. "The people of the Anglo-Saxon era," it says, in a snooty sort of a way, "although converted to Christianity, believed in dragons, monsters and spirits. Such beliefs persisted into the medieval period and are reflected in the art of the time." Of course you and I know better, is what it's saying, under the posh language.

Well, as I've said before, that's as may be. Everyone's entitled to their own opinion.

There were these two boys living in the village, in a house not so far from the church. We'll call them Joe and Pete, though that's not their real names. Brothers, they were. Well, they grew up in this house in the middle of the village between the pub and the butcher's. It was an old house—that goes without saying. This is an old village and some of the houses go back two or three hundred years and maybe more. It was a bit cramped, though, for a growing family, and eventually their dad decided to make a bit more space by turning the old scullery at the back into another room. They had to do a fair bit of work to make it fit to use, and one of the things they had to do was lay a new floor. And what do you think they found when they took up the old stone flags? A darn great well, going straight down into the ground, deep and black so you couldn't see the bottom nor even get an idea where it went. There was no water in it, that was for sure—they lowered a bucket down and it came up dry as a bone. Of course the boys thought this was a right bit of fun, having a well under the house, and they wanted it left open, but their dad wasn't having any of that, and he made a round cover for it, hinged, with a padlock, and he shut it down and locked it up and read them a lecture about how they weren't ever to meddle with it. And that, so far as he was concerned, was that.

And so it might have been for the boys too if it hadn't been for the noises. They heard them first only a day or two after their dad had fixed up the cover. A kind of a moaning, it was, far away down there under the ground. A sad kind of a noise, like the sea when you hear it at night, lying in bed, or trees in the wind, and every now and then there'd be something else too. It sounded like scratching.

The boys got their heads down and lay with their ears stuck to the cover of the well, trying to fathom out what might be going on down there. Fathom's the right word for it, too—you could hardly see the bottom even with a torch, it was that deep.

"Rats," said Joe.

"Whoever heard of rats that cry?" said Pete. "And what are they living on? Air?"

"Maybe there's a person down there," said Joe in a trembly voice, "stuck!"

Pete didn't even bother to answer that one.

Well, I daresay you know as much about human nature as I do, and the human nature of boys in particular, and you've guessed what happened next. Their dad hadn't been as crafty as he thought he had about putting his keys away and it didn't take them that long to find the right one and get that padlock undone. They got the cover off and then they lay on their

stomachs and stared down into the darkness, though
a bit gingerly, mind, because they were both scared,
though they weren't going to let on to each other that
they were.

"I wouldn't like to fall down there," said Joe,
keeping a good hold of the scullery floor.

"We're not daft, are we?" said Pete.

They couldn't see anything, just a round circle of
darkness, so they got a torch, and the torch made a
yellow hole in the darkness and they could see the
sides, quite straight and all slippery-damp, and they
could just make out the bottom. And then they heard
the noise again. Sigh. Scratch. Sigh.

"Suppose we dropped something down?" said Joe
in a whisper.

So they got the end of a loaf of bread from the larder, that had gone mouldy, and they dropped it down the well and they could just see it land at the bottom and sit there, crumb-sized.

And something came out of the side at the bottom, a kind of a claw, scaly they thought, and some sort of a long snout, and the bread disappeared, and they could hear a munching noise, far away down there.

They got some chicken bones from the dustbin, and dropped them down too, and a pile of potato peelings and the porridge Pete hadn't eaten for breakfast, and all that went the same way as the bread. And so did a handkerchief that Joe dropped by mistake, so they got the old telephone directory that had been thrown out, and that disappeared too, and so did an empty dog-food tin and a cereal packet.

They knew what they'd got down there, all right. After all, they knew that wall-painting in the church well enough, didn't they? They'd sat underneath it every Sunday morning as far back as they could re-member. Besides, they'd seen the creature—or a bit of it.

"It's smaller than you'd think," said Pete. "Not much bigger than our Tim, I'd say." (Tim was their dog—a mongrel that could pass for some sort of retriever.)

Joe nodded. "Just goes to show," he said. "There's a lot of blowing things up in those old stories. Ravaging the countryside and that. A thing that size couldn't do much ravaging."

"It was starving, poor thing," said Pete indignantly.

They chucked some more bits and pieces down and presently the thing stopped its noises and there was a deep peaceful silence down there so they put the cover back on and went to bed.

Over the next few days they had a bit of a think about things. They reckoned the dragon must have been hibernating ("For hundreds of years most likely," said Pete. "I'll bet they live just about for ever, like those giant tortoises.") and that all the clattering around over his head with the new floor being put down had stirred him up again. They also reckoned that he must be living in a hole or tunnel or something that opened off from the bottom of the well—"Funny kind of well . . ." said Pete.

Anyway, they were tickled pink at the thought of what they'd got. Talk about pets—it knocked white mice and hamsters and budgies into a cocked hat, that did. They even looked up dragons in the dictionary, to see if there were any tips about upkeep, but all it said was that a dragon was a mythical monster (and they knew better than that: "Mythical, my foot," said Joe scornfully) or, alternatively, a lizard of the genus *draco*, having on each flank a broad, wing-like membrane. . . . And then there were some bits of poetry— "His Armes spred wider than a Dragons Wings . . . ,"

"Swift, swift, you Dragons of the night. . . ." Nothing about diet or habits. The only trouble was, they couldn't tell anyone about it. One word to their parents, and the rat-catcher would have been called in, or the RSPCA, or the fire brigade, and that would have been the end of it all. "Put it away in a cage, they would," said Joe, "if we let them get their hands on it," and Pete added with a shudder, "Or get it stuffed." And I daresay they were right. I've never been surprised the Loch Ness monster takes care to keep itself to itself—it knows where it's well off, that one.

Well, for a week or so it was all a bit of a lark. Every evening, soon as they were sure no one was about, they'd take the lid off the well and give the dragon whatever they'd managed to scrounge. It was nocturnal, you see—during the day there was never a peep out of it, but as soon as it was dark they'd hear it, sighing and scratching and worse, and it would go on until it had had as much as it wanted to eat, and then it would go to sleep and there'd be peace and quiet. This was all very well, but the trouble was that its appetite was growing all the time, and the hungrier it was the more noise it made. They were getting properly worried, I can tell you, for fear their mum and dad would hear it. Luckily their dad always had the television on in the evening, and their mum would be clattering about with the dishes and that, so there was a fair bit of noise going on anyway. But even so they didn't know how much longer they could go on like this.

It knew when feeding-time was now, you see, and it would be scrabbling around down there, and howling, even before they got the lid off, and it would go on all the time they were dropping things down until it reckoned it had had a fair deal, and then it would settle down for the night. Getting enough stuff for it was taking up most of their spare time nowadays. They knew all the neighbours' dustbins like old friends, and they'd hang around the butcher's, picking up what

they could in the way of bones and staring longingly at the sides of mutton and pork. "One of those," Joe would say, "and you'd have it sleeping for a week." And they'd whip what they could from the school rubbish bins by way of waste-paper and empty boxes. The fact was, you see, the creature would eat anything. The nastier the better, it seemed. Empty tins it loved— you'd hear it scrunching away down there, and the boys had got in the way of rattling a couple of tins to let it know they were opening up, though they came to regret that because they'd got it a bit too well-trained after a bit, as you might say, and you only had to accidentally drop a tin to start it off racketing around. Fish that had gone really bad it particularly liked, and it must have had a keen sense of smell because it would know way off when there was something choice in that line coming down.

It wasn't long before the boys hit on the idea of collecting the odd armful of stuff from the old rubbish tip at the edge of the village. The rubbish tip was a bit of a sore point with everyone—it was smelly and an eyesore and every now and then somebody would write an indignant letter to the paper and say it was time the Rural District Council did something about it, and the Rural District Council would write an official letter back saying it was just going to, and then everybody would forget about it for another six months. Well, the boys picked up some delicacies there by way of empty lemonade bottles and rusty bed-springs, and they were just setting off home when they met an old chap who lived nearby who'd been emptying stuff into the tip and got his barrow stuck down a hole that had opened up in the path. They helped him get the barrow out and he thanked them and then chatted a bit and he told them something they hadn't ever known before which was that the tip had been an old mine once, way back, and there were shafts running off from it, underground, all over the place.

"Go right under the village, they do," he said. "Tunnels, all over. Like a 'unneycomb, it is," and he pointed out a spot where, sure enough, there was a black hole, like a giant rabbit-hole, at one side of the tip.

Are you with me? I'll bet you are—one jump ahead, like Joe and Pete were soon as they heard that. Tunnels? Right under the village? Wells coming up in people's houses?

"That wasn't ever a well," said Joe, and they looked at each other, and there was no need to say any more.

The problem, and I daresay you've spotted it too, was how they were to teach the dragon that it had to go to the other end of the tunnel to get its meal. Their house was only about four hundred yards or so, direct, from the tip, and they reckoned that the tunnel—if there was one, and they were gambling on that—would go straight. So it wasn't that far, but the creature had got set in its ways now, as you might say, and they couldn't see at first how they were going to get it doing something different. There were two things, though, that they reckoned would come in handy. One was the creature's sense of smell, and the other was the little bit of training they'd given it with rattling tins together.

They got some fish from the fishmonger's dustbin, and let it mature in the garden hedge till it was good and high, and then, one dusk, just about the time they usually fed the dragon, they went down to the tip. Round the side they went, till they were on the over-hang above that hole I mentioned earlier, and they dropped the fish down in front of the hole, and then

they lowered a bunch of tins on the end of a bit of string, and rattled them as hard as they'd go. They rattled for a good minute or so, and then they dashed over to the far side of the tip, out of the way, just to be on the safe side, because you couldn't be sure what its temper might be like after all that time underground, and they waited.

It was almost dark. So dark they could only just see the mouth of the hole as a black splodge. Nothing happened—for a minute and then another minute and then another. And then they saw the black splodge get bigger and half of it split off into something dark that moved away from the hole, a bit uncertain, as if it didn't quite know what was up, and they saw it nose around among the old prams and the cardboard boxes and the mountains of rusty tins. And presently, clear as clear, they heard a scrunching noise. A contented kind of a noise. Like a dog that's got his dinner, and plenty of it.

And that's just about the end of the story. The boys went home, and they never heard anything under the scullery floor again. Old Bert Timms, though, whose cottage backs on to the tip—the chap with the barrow that they met that time—he used to look out of his window of an evening and he'd see and hear things in the tip that would surprise a good many people, but he never used to mention it. He'd lived in the village all his life, had Bert, and his dad before him, and his dad's dad before that, and he knew there's a time for talking and a time for keeping your mouth shut. And I'll tell you another thing too—the Rural District Council never did do anything about the tip, and the funny thing is that all these years people have been chucking their rubbish into it and it never does seem to get any bigger.

If you're wondering what happened to the boys— well, Pete went overseas when he grew up but Joe, he's still around these parts.

Time Trouble

When I was nine I came to an arrangement with a grandfather clock; it was disastrous. Never trust a clock. Believe me—I know. I'll tell you about it.

I was in the hall of our house, all by myself. Except for the clock. I'd just come in from school. The clock said ten past four. And I said, out loud, because I was fed up and cross as two sticks, "I'd give anything to have this afternoon all over again."

"Would you now," said a voice. "That's interesting."

There was no one there. I swear. Mum was out shopping and my brother Brian was off playing with his mate down the road. The voice came from the clock. I looked it in the eye and it looked back, the way they do. Well, they've got faces, haven't they? Faces look.

"I deal in time, as it happens," the clock went on. "Had some bad time, have you?"

Funny stuff, time. I mean, it can be good or bad, and you're always being told not to lose it and we all spend it and some of us kill it. You can have overtime and half-time and summer time and the time of your life. And there's always next time. And my time's my own, so's yours.

I nodded.

"Sometimes," said the clock, "I can lend a hand." It twitched one, from eleven minutes past four to twelve minutes past. "Tell me all, then."

So I told. About how at dinner I was in a bad mood because of having a fight with Brian and when Mum kept going on at me about something I kept thinking "Oh, shut up!" only unfortunately what was meant to be a think got said out loud accidentally so then Mum was in a very bad mood indeed with me and I got no pudding. And then on the way back to school Brian and I had another fight and my new pencil case got kicked into a puddle and all dirtied over. And we were late and Mrs Harris told us off. And I answered back accidentally and so she sent me to the headmaster and he told me off even more. And I had to stay in at break.

And Martin Chalmers nicked my rubber so I had to keep asking for it back so Mrs Harris told me off again. And I had to go to the end of the classroom and sit by myself. And on the way home I got hold of Martin Chalmers and we had an argument resulting in me falling over and my pocket money dropping out of my pocket and ten pence getting lost.

"Tough," said the clock. "I see what you mean. Well—here's a deal. You have this afternoon back and I'll have next Wednesday."

"Next Wednesday?"

"Next Wednesday. Your next Wednesday afternoon."

"But I don't know yet what's going to happen next Wednesday," I objected.

"Quite," said the clock. "It's a risk. Well—take it or leave it."

I thought. What's one Wednesday afternoon, out of all the Wednesday afternoons you've got? I mean, on the whole one Wednesday afternoon's much like another.

"O.K," I said. "And I have this one again?"

The clock made its whirring noise for quarter past four. "That's right, my lad. See if you can make a better job of it."

You're not going to believe this. There I was at dinner all over again, in a bad mood just like before, only this time when Mum started going on at me I

66

didn't say anything, I just sat. And then somehow accidentally my leg shot out and it kicked Brian and Brian yelled and his milk got spilled and Mum got in a proper temper and not only did I get no pudding but I got no seconds either. On the way back to school I thought. Right . . . And when Brian started trying to trip me up I didn't trip back but I started running on ahead. And a paving stone got in my way and I fell over and my new pencil case went into the road and a car went over it and all the pencils were broken and the biro with six colours was bent so it wouldn't work any more. And we were late and I didn't answer Mrs Harris back but I kept trying to explain only she called it interrupting and the headmaster came in and heard and I had to stay in at break and help tidy up the infant class as a punishment and Brian and Martin Chalmers

kept looking in at the window and making faces and I made faces back. And I got on one of the desks to see out better. And put dirty footmarks on it. And Mrs Harris came in. So I had to spend all afternoon at the end of the classroom by myself. And when the bell went I rushed off before Martin Chalmers came out and I was so fed up I went into the corner shop for a Twix. And you're not going to believe this. My money had all gone out of my pocket. Twenty-eight pence from last Saturday. It must have dropped out when I fell over before.

There I was in the hall again. With the clock. Furious. I said, "It was *worse*. I want the first one back again. That way, at least I'd have my money and the pencils and the biro with six colours."

"No way," said the clock. "A deal's a deal." And it just stood there, ticking. That was all it did for the next five days.

I wondered what would happen, when it came to Wednesday. What happened was this. Brian and I came home from school for dinner, just as usual. We ate it, just as usual. Mum said, "Off you go, boys," just as usual. We started getting on our anoraks. The phone rang. The clock struck one. Mum said, "Wonder who that is . . ." She went to answer the phone.

. . . And the next thing I knew the clock was striking seven and I was in the kitchen again looking at a plate of supper that I didn't want. I felt a bit sick.

I said, "I feel a bit sick."

"I'm not surprised," said Mum.

"You shouldn't have had the peach melba bombe as well as the vanilla with chocolate sauce," said Brian.

I looked at him.

"Cor . . ." he went on, in a sort of contented, reflective voice. "Weren't the Jumbo Beefburgers *smashing* . . ."

I didn't say a word. An awful, suspicious feeling began to creep over me.

Brian was talking about something else now. "Remember the bit when the spaceships all started crashing into each other? That was *fantastic*. And when the robots all came out of the volcano?"

Mum had gone out of the back door for something. I thought hard. I said, cautiously, "What sort of an afternoon was it, would you say?"

"What sort of an afternoon!" cried Brian. "It was just amazing! Well, you were *there*, you dope! I mean, it's not just any old afternoon that Uncle Jim suddenly rings up and says he's over this way and he'd like to take us out and he talks Mum into letting us miss school and he comes in his new *sports* car with the *roof* down all the way and . . . Well, you were *there*. Hey—remember the bit in the cartoon when they all fell over the cliff!"

I swallowed. "Yeah . . . Sure." After a moment I said, "It was *Space Victory*, was it, the film?"

He stared at me. " 'Course it was *Space Victory*, idiot. *Space Victory*, what we've been wanting to see for *years*. Remember the bit when . . ."

" 'Course," I snarled through clenched teeth. I went on, wishing I wasn't. "What's that place called—the Wimpy Bar, is it?"

"Wimpy Bar!" cried Brian. "Some Wimpy Bar! That was the Plaza Steak House, you nut! Hey—bet you haven't ever had three helpings of chips before!"

I groaned. I wished he'd shut up, but I went on listening.

"*And* beefburgers *and* bacon rolls *and* Coca-Cola *and* three different kinds of ice cream *and* crisps *and* milk shakes. Actually," he said, pushing his plate to one side, "I feel a tiny bit sick too. I'll just *think* about it all. Remember the bit when . . ."

I went out into the hall, banging the door. I stood in front of the clock. "Did you *know*?" I demanded.

"What's that?" said the clock, bland as you like.

"Did you *know* that it wouldn't just be an ordinary school afternoon? Did you *know* Uncle Jim would come . . . and . . . *Space Victory* . . . *three* helpings of chips . . ." I spluttered. I couldn't go on.

The clock ticked away, evasive. "I said it would be a risk, didn't I? Funny stuff, time. Doesn't always do to mess about with it."

"It was your idea," I said sulkily.

"Look," said the clock. "I was just going about my

normal business, dealing in time. If you don't like what's in the paper you don't complain to the news-agent, do you?"

I glared at it.

"I just keep track of it, right? See it's moving along at the proper rate, all that kind of thing. One bit's the same as another, far as I'm concerned. The quality's your problem—doesn't interest me."

I said, "I want my Wednesday afternoon back."

The clock considered. "Mmn. That would be a new arrangement. Different deal altogether. Let's see now. How about next, um, next December the twenty-fifth?"

"*Christmas Day?*" I yelled.

"Suit yourself." If a clock can be said to shrug, it did so. I thought about *Space Victory* and Uncle Jim's sports car with the roof down and three different kinds of ice cream. I mean, the whole point about having a good time is that it's good when you have it and it's still good when you remember it. And I couldn't re-member any of this; I'd had it and not known about it then and I still didn't know about it. I thought about next Christmas. Half the point of good things that are going to come is that you know you've still got them coming. No, the clock wasn't going to get Christmas.

"Tomorrow morning?" I offered. After all, an ordinary old Thursday morning . . .

"I've got lots of those," said the clock.

"I thought you said it was all the same to you?" I said craftily.

"Cheeky!" snapped the clock. "You watch out or I'll stop. And then where will you be?"

I didn't know the answer to that, so I said nothing.

"Tell you what. I'll be generous. I'll just have the time you waste. Now that you'll never miss."

I thought. I thought, I bet there's a snag somewhere. I didn't trust that clock an inch now. After a moment I said, "O.K. But just for next week."

"You're so sharp you'll cut yourself. A month."

"Two weeks."

The clock whirred. "All right, then. Done. Off you go. Have fun."

And it struck one and there I was in the kitchen and the phone was ringing and Mum saying, "Wonder who that is . . ."

And Uncle Jim came and he took us off in the sports car with the roof down and we went to *Space Victory* and then to the Plaza Steak House and I had two Jumbo Beefburgers and three helpings of chips and three different kinds of ice cream and Coca-Cola and . . . It was all exactly like I knew it was going to be. Oh, yes, it was pretty good, I mean it was fantastic in a way but the edge had kind of gone off it. It wasn't nearly as fantastic as it ought to have been. Half the point of a good time is not knowing what's coming next. So *Space Victory* wasn't as amazing as I thought it was

going to be and the beefburgers were all right but not much more and I kept thinking it wasn't as good as it was supposed to be which made it worse.

And I was stuck with the deal. I bet you're wondering about that. So was I. I mean, who's to say whether you're wasting time or not? Mothers and teachers have one idea about wasting time; people like me have another. Fact is, if you're anything like me you probably do quite a lot of smooching around doing nothing in particular, sort of waiting for something to happen. I s'pose you *could* call that wasting time, if you insisted.

The clock, evidently, did. It was the worst two weeks I've ever had. I'm telling you. Every time I stopped doing something, such as eating a meal or having a bath or doing maths or walking to school or getting dressed, everything just went blank. And there I'd be again in the middle of the next thing. It was like being in a speeded-up film. It was all go; there was never a moment's peace. I was exhausted. There I'd be cleaning my teeth and I'd dawdle a bit and try out a few faces in the bathroom mirror and then wham! I'd find myself downstairs and out of the front door on the way to school. Or I'd stop in the middle of a sum to have a bit of a think and the think would begin to get sort of vague and wandery—you know the way they do—and whoosh! there I'd be sweating away again at the sum and the bell would be going for break. I didn't know if I was coming or going. The only thing to be said for it was that the days went by double-quick. Suddenly the two weeks were over and everything slowed up and went back to normal. Goodness—what a relief! The first thing I did was go into the hall and stand in front of the clock and do absolutely nothing, for five whole minutes, on purpose. I'd have gone on longer, just to annoy it, except that I was getting bored. I started to go upstairs.

"All right," said the clock. "You've made your point."

I glared at the clock and the clock looked back, blank. No, not blank: smug.

"Look," it said. "Maybe I could interest you in a personal arrangement. Just you and me. Might be fun. How about you . . ."

"NO!" I shouted.

Princess by Mistake

A long time ago, when I was young, on a Wednesday afternoon, a very strange thing happened to me. So strange, you probably won't believe it. That's up to you. Anyway, this is what happened.

I know it was a Wednesday, because we always went to the library on Wednesday afternoons, my mother and my sister Sally and I. And all the way home from the library my sister Sally and I had a fight. We squabbled our way down the High Street and past the churchyard and over the bridge and by the time we got home our mother was in a proper temper with us and I don't blame her either. I can't remember now what we were quarrelling about—I think it was for something to do as much as anything. Sally said I'd got a stupid lot of books—they were all about aeroplanes which was what I was interested in at the time—and I said the ones she had were boring and babyish. Fairy stories, they were. Truth to tell, I rather liked fairy stories myself but I wanted to annoy Sally, who had a craze on them. Load of old rubbish! I jeered. Kings and queens! Fairy godmothers! Princesses! And we went on fighting each other all around the house till suddenly my mother had had enough and she turned us out. She bundled us out of the front door and told us not to come back till we could behave sensibly.

So off we wandered, up the street, arguing away about one thing and another at the tops of our voices. We were quite enjoying ourselves, really: it was a way of passing the time. We argued about who could run fastest and jump highest and swim best and then we got on to each other's personal appearance. Sally passed a few remarks about my freckles and I had a go at her long fair hair, of which she was excessively proud. "Goldilocks!" I shouted. "S'pose you think you're the queen of the fairies! S'pose you think you're a princess!" That was unwise, because Sally was very vain about her hair. She went bright scarlet and flew at me, and we rolled into the ditch together, scuffling.

It was the ditch outside Mr Crackington-Smith's

garden. Mr Crackington-Smith was an elderly bachelor with a reputation for being difficult. He kept himself to himself and had awkward relations with his neighbours. Sally and I were so busy with our fight that neither of us saw him watching us over his gate, nor heard him say, "Will you kindly stop making that unpleasant noise outside my house." Presently, though, we stopped for a breather and looked up and saw him, scowling at us. He said, "Go away!"

And we sat there, all muddy and red in the face, and Sally said, very quietly, so quietly you wouldn't have thought he could possibly have heard, "Why should we?"

Mr Crackington-Smith said, "Because I'm telling you to. And if you don't," he went on, with a positive gleam in his eye, "I shall remove you."

We stared. Mr Crackington-Smith was quite a small man; we were rather large children. We heaved ourselves out of the ditch in silence, and shuffled about at the edge of the road. In fact we were just about to go, but Sally couldn't resist saying—to me, rudely, in a half-whisper—"I s'pose he thinks he's a magician or something?"

Mr Crackington-Smith took a pair of secateurs out of his pocket and started doing something to a rose. "As a matter of fact I am," he said calmly.

I sniggered.

Which was one of the stupidest things I ever did.

(I trust that by now you are properly shocked at what badly-behaved, ill-mannered and unperceptive children we were, my sister Sally and I.)

After that everything happened at once. There was a great crack of thunder, and a flash of lightning. For exactly half a minute it rained very small toads; a number of black cats appeared on the garden wall and squalled horribly; broomsticks clattered around us like autumn leaves, and there was a loud thud of horse's hooves. Sally gave a kind of squeak, and I looked round to see her being heaved, kicking and struggling, on to the back of an enormous black horse by a huge figure in full armour wearing a crown. "Help!" she bellowed. I just had time to see, as the person arranged

her across the saddle in front of him, thrashing about like a fish in a net, that she was done up in full fairy-story princess gear—long frock, flowers in her hair, the lot—and then the person dug his spurs into the horse and away they went down the road, sparks flying from the tarmac, Sally yelling blue murder.

"Well," said Mr Crackington-Smith smugly, "satisfied?"

I said faintly: "What's he going to do with her?"

Mr Crackington-Smith was busy with his pruning now. "Oh, the usual stuff, I expect," he said. "Impenetrable dungeon with rats and snakes and all that. Standard fate of princesses. You'd better get on with it, hadn't you?"

"Get on with what?"

"Rescuing her, you stupid boy," said Mr Crackington-Smith irritably. He glanced at me and added, "I suppose we'd better give you a bit of the normal equipment."

There was a hiss and a clunk, and I found a very large heavy sword stuck firmly into my belt. I took a step forward and tripped over it. "It's too long," I said sullenly.

"Fusspot," said Mr Crackington-Smith. He waved his secateurs in the air and the sword shrank six inches. "Well," he said, "all the best." He put the secateurs in his pocket and began to walk towards his house.

I said desperately, "What do I *do*?"

Mr Crackington-Smith looked over his shoulder. "Oh, for goodness sake!" he said. "Just the straightforward routine! Impossible tasks; dragons and ogres and whatnot; spells; everybody else having an unfair advantage. Just do your best. The sword's a bit blunt, by the way. Oh, and I daresay you might find these come in handy too." I felt something in my hands and looked down to find myself holding, in one, a packet of gobstoppers and in the other a folded-up comic. "How do I *start?*" I yelled.

His voice floated back through the closing front-door. "The Blue Star Garage, of course. He'll be turning that clapped-out old nag into a car by now. You'll know which by the usual signs."

The door slammed.

I set off down the road, the sword banging uncomfortably against my leg with every step. I passed one or two people I knew, but nobody gave me a second look: whatever was happening was happening only to Sally and me. The sword slapped my leg and glittered in the sunshine.

I reached the garage. There were several cars being filled up with petrol, and a red van. The van-driver had his back to me, but the van had large black letters on it that said CASTLE DESPAIR PEST CONTROL SERVICE TEL. DRAGONSWICK 469. There was a sound of banging and shouting from inside the closed doors. The driver turned to look at me, with an evil grin; I saw the glint of chain mail under his overalls. He got into the van, slammed the door, and drove off at high speed. I stood there, staring after it.

"Gracious me!" said a voice. "Don't just stand there, boy. Get on and *do* something."

I looked round. There was no one about, but on top of one of the petrol pumps was a small green frog. Which, you must admit, is not at all the place you'd expect to find a small green frog. It all fitted. I said to it, "How?"

"Put me in your pocket," said the frog. "I can see you're an amateur—you'll never cope with this on your own. Ouch! Don't squeeze! Now—we need transport. Hop on that motorbike."

"But I don't know how to ride it," I protested, "and anyway, I'm not old enough . . ."

"Oh, don't quibble," said the frog impatiently.

I got on to the bike—it was one of those great big fast Japanese ones—and it won't surprise you to hear, I imagine, that it went off just like that, obedient as a horse. I didn't have to ride it—it just went. And nobody looked up nor stared at me nor turned a hair; it was as though we were invisible, me and the bike and that frog in my pocket.

We roared down the road, and just round the first bend we caught sight of the tail of the red van disappearing over the top of the hill. "There he goes!" said the frog. "Step it up a bit!"

I said, breathlessly, as the motorbike hurtled up to seventy miles an hour, "Who is he, anyway?"

"Gracious," said the frog, "how ignorant can you get! He's the Black King, isn't he? The fear and dread of all. Stops at nothing. Every crime in the book. Collects princesses. Got twenty-nine of them locked up at his place. Your sister's a princess, I take it?"

"No," I said, "she's Sally Smithers of 14 Winterton Road."

"Ah," said the frog with interest, "case of mistaken identity, then. Must be the hair that did it. He wouldn't stop to find out, anyway. Whoa there! They went thataway . . . ."

We screamed round another bend and suddenly, where there ought to have been the rather ordinary view of the outskirts of the next town, with rows of semis and a few shops and a school and that kind of thing, there was a great sweep of pine forest, with mountains behind and, bang in the middle, a huge castle straight off a pantomime back-cloth—all towers and turrets and slit windows and drawbridges and what-have-you. The red van was just whisking over a drawbridge and in at the gate. We dashed after it, and as we arrived a few hundred yards from the castle walls there was a convulsive heaving of the ground and out of it sprang a thick undergrowth of thorn bushes, as impassable as anything you ever saw. "Here we go," said the frog, "up to his old tricks.

Well, we can scupper that one, I reckon. Where's your sword?"

"Here," I said. I brandished it around uncertainly, and, would you believe it, even as I did so the blessed thing turned into a great big mowing machine, like my dad's only three times the size, with THORNMASTER SUPREME in black letters on the handle. "Let her go!" yelled the frog, and I tore into the brambles with the mower and in no time at all we had cleared a path right up to the castle entrance. The motorbike had vanished.

"Help!" cried a small voice, from somewhere far away, and looking down the cliff-like walls of the castle, as they plunged down the side of a ravine, I saw a thin red flag fluttering from a barred window. Sally's hair-ribbon. "Help!" called her voice, thin and pathetic. "Help! Snakes! Spiders! I want to go home."

"Not to worry, my dear," bawled the frog (he had a remarkably loud voice for one so small), "rescue operation under way! Press on . . ."

The drawbridge was still down. I hurried across it, and just as we reached the open gateway there was the most appalling roar and out leapt the largest dog you ever saw in your life, with—yes, you've guessed it—eight heads, all splayed out from a great iron collar with a tag saying BOHEMIAN SECURITY SERVICES—YOUR PROPERTY IS OUR CONCERN. I took six paces backwards. "Get down, you brute!" said the frog. "Quick—tranquillise it!"

I said, "What?" and then I remembered the packet of gobstoppers in my pocket. I pulled them out and hurled one at each head, and the dog snapped them up and stood there sucking and gulping and quick as a flash we were past it and into the great courtyard of the castle. I stared round in perplexity; there were a great many entrances, and a nasty smell of mushrooms, and black ravens all over the place, shuffling up and down the parapets. The frog, from my pocket, said, "I predict an ogre. Keep on your toes. Be prepared for evasive action."

I slipped through the nearest doorway. Inside, there was a kind of entrance hall, very cold and damp, amazingly, the doors of a lift, with a panel of buttons beside it saying FIRST FLOOR AND BANQUETING HALL; WEST TOWER AND BOILING–OIL CHAMBER; BEDROOMS 1–489; THRONE ROOM, and, finally, DUNGEONS AND GUEST ROOMS.

"So far so good," said the frog.

I stepped forward and pressed the button marked DUNGEONS, and just as I did so there was a kind of howling from down a long dark stone passage, rather like the noise of an approaching plane, getting louder and nearer all the time. "Thought so . . ." said the frog. "Watch out!" and there in front of us was an immense ogre, with a great head of shaggy red hair, dressed in sacking, armed with a club studded with six-inch nails. The frog whispered, "Play it cool—they're not very bright, usually."

I said politely, "Good morning."

"Wurra-wurra-wurra-hhrumph . . . HOP IT!" bellowed the ogre, advancing, and waving his club around.

I side-stepped hastily and said, "I won't disturb anyone. I was just going to pop down to the dungeons and rescue my sister."

"Wassat?" said the ogre, scratching his head. He didn't seem all that quick on the uptake.

The frog poked his nose out of my pocket and said,

"No need to bother yourself with small fry like us—a fine strapping fellow like you."

"Grrrr . . . !" said the ogre, flexing his muscles with ostentation. "Thirteen foot five in me socks; forty-one stone six pounds."

"Fantastic!" said the frog, nudging me. I edged towards the lift again, and pushed the button.

"Oy-oy . . ." growled the ogre. "Whaddya-think-yer-doing . . . HOP IT! SCRAM!"

"Amazing . . ." said the frog. "Thirteen foot five! Ever thought of tossing the caber? Javelin throwing? Olympic wrestling, that kind of thing?"

But it was the wrong approach. The ogre glared and began to rumble threateningly, "You think I'm some kinda dumb stoopid muscle man?"—I pressed the lift button as hard as I could—"You think I'm a bit thick or somefing? I'm a thinking man, I tell yer, I read books, I . . ."

"Absolutely," said the frog, "quite so. Obvious to anyone."

I groped in my pocket. "Here," I said, "present for you . . ." and I flung the comic at the ogre, as hard as I could.

He grabbed hold of it and a great beaming smile spread over his face. "Aaah!" he said. "Wow! Cor! Smashing!" He began to turn his pages over with his enormous fingers, and at that moment there was a whirr and a click and the lift doors slid open.

"Quick!" said the frog, and I shot into the lift and slammed my hand down on the START button. The doors slid shut again and the lift plunged down.

It stopped. The doors opened. I got out, cautiously.

There was darkness, and stone walls streaming with water, and things that slithered off into the gloom, and flappings and squeakings and unpleasant smells. "Press on," said the frog, "this is the crunch. Himself will be somewhere about, I don't doubt."

I stumbled forward, calling, "Sally! Sally!" And

after a minute or two, distantly, we heard a faint, answering voice. A number of faint, answering voices.

I rushed on, calling Sally's name, and the answering cries got closer and closer until at last I groped my way round a corner and there in front was a great padlocked door with an iron grille at the top, and Sally's face peering through it, shrieking, "Help! Get me out of here!"

"Move over," said the frog, "this is where I come in. Allowed one trick up your sleeve—it's all part of the game." And with that, he sprang out of my pocket, landed on the padlock, and turned himself into a small iron file which sliced through the metal quick as a flash. The padlock fell off, and the frog, looking a little sore around the mouth, reappeared poking his nose out of my pocket.

I flung the door open, and there was Sally, and a whole lot of other girls, all weeping and wailing and all in princess outfits. They fell on me in the most embarrassing way. And then all of a sudden there was a clatter of heavy footsteps in the passage outside. "Here we go!" said the frog. "It's up to you now! One thing—his backhand's weak."

It was the Black King. He sprang at me, armoured from top to toe, and I sprang back, with my sword in my hand (it said THORNMASTER SUPREME on the handle now—there'd been a slip-up somewhere). We fought round and round and up and down and to and fro, with all the princesses cheering like mad, and twice I had him down and once he had me down, and then, just as I thought I couldn't go on a minute longer, he gave a great howl and a banshee wail and there was a puff of horrible black sulphurous smoke, and he was gone.

We all streamed out of the castle, Sally and I and the princesses and the frog in my pocket. The princesses all said, "Thank you *ever* so much, that was *really* kind . . ." and went dashing off in all directions, and Sally and I leapt onto the motorbike, which had reappeared again just outside the castle, and we roared off too and . . .

There we were on the edge of the road outside Mr Crackington-Smith's house. No motorbike, no frog, no sword, Sally in jeans and a T-shirt again. We looked at each other. Neither of us said anything. We walked home, very slowly, and we didn't say a thing but every now and then we glanced at each other, quick, and then looked away again. I knew. Sally knew. We still do. We don't talk about it, even now. It was a funny thing to happen, wasn't it—on a Wednesday afternoon. As I said, you'll have to take it or leave it, it's up to you—I'm just telling you what happened.

A Flock of Gryphons

It is not only human beings who use churches and cathedrals—you'll have noticed that. Birds do, too. Look carefully, next time you're in front of a cathedral and somewhere, perched on the head of a statue, poking out of a gutter, you'll see an untidy mass of sticks: a pigeon's nest.

Westminster Abbey, in London, is no exception. London pigeons, let me tell you, are very set in their ways. They don't move easily. They stay in the same part for generations. Trafalgar Square pigeons wouldn't be seen dead south of the river; Westminster

Abbey pigeons consider themselves a cut above the St Paul's lot. And those two, mind, are the most superior roosts in London. The pigeons who nest high up on the west front of the Abbey claim that they have inherited the right since the time of William the Conqueror. Between you and me, that's pushing it a bit, but it's true enough that some of them could trace their nests back to Queen Victoria, or even to the battle of Waterloo.

It's an odd place to be raised, for a young pigeon. Think of it—up there among the statues of kings and saints and the gargoyles and the fantastic birds and beasts that cathedrals have all over them. Very fantastic indeed, some of them are—dragons and serpents and fishes and I don't know what. It wouldn't be surprising if a bit of confusion arose—if funny things happened—if the parent pigeons, sitting there amongst all that, became a little disordered.

The pair with which we're concerned, though, would never have admitted that. Perfectly ordinary, law-abiding folk they considered themselves, going about their business in a quiet way, raising one brood every year, spending their days on the nest or feeding their offspring or pottering around Parliament Square gardens being polite to the tourists like any responsible London pigeon. Nevertheless, it was they who began it all. Or it was in their nest that it all began.

At first everything seemed quite normal. The two

eggs hatched, on time, without fuss, and there were the usual pink wriggling chicks. It wasn't until about the third or fourth week that the mother pigeon had a suspicion things weren't as they should be.

She said, "You know, there's something funny about this year's lot."

The father peered into the nest. "They're always ugly at this stage, dear." And indeed they were, as you'll know if you've ever seen a young pigeon: featherless except for a few half-hearted quills, huge-headed and wide-mouthed and a nasty mottled pink and grey colour.

"These are different," insisted the mother. "They give me a funny feeling." Her voice sank to a whisper. "I think they're growing *tails* . . ."

After a few days the father began to share her doubts. He called in an old wise pigeon, one of the leaders of the flock, privileged for many years to roost on the head of Edward the Confessor. The two of them studied the contents of the nest. At last the old pigeon spoke.

"Well, I hardly know what to say. You were quite right to be concerned."

The mother began to weep. "It's not my fault. I've done all the right things. I've fed them and sat on them . . ."

The old pigeon sighed. "I'm sure you shouldn't blame yourself. It could have happened to anyone. Put it down to the weather. Or the government. Or all those satellites whizzing around up above."

"What *are* they?" demanded the father.

"What you've got there," said the old pigeon, "is a pair of gryphons."

The mother gave a little shriek.

"Small gryphons, but gryphons without a doubt. Head and wings of an eagle, tail of a serpent, body of a lion. These look like ending up feathered, which is unusual, but the rest is pretty well standard."

"Eagle . . . !" said the mother faintly.

"Pigeon-sized, they'll be, that's for sure. And unique. There's never been anything like it. Unknown to science. But I can see it's upsetting for you."

It certainly was. The parent pigeons continued to feed and look after their peculiar offspring; the mother was so distressed and embarrassed that she was unable to talk to any of her friends and neighbours. Consequently it was a few days before rumours reached her that all was not well in other Abbey nests. "It's not just us," whispered her husband. "It's happened to some of the others," and I'm afraid that, pigeon nature being much like human nature, they both felt a faint sense of relief. At least they weren't embarrassed alone.

Their gryphons were the first to leave the nest. As soon as they were fully fledged, and so large that they were almost falling out anyway, they began to flap their wings and stretch their necks and then one bright

June morning they both took off and flapped and floated down from the top of the Abbey, high above the buses and the cars and the bustling people, down through the trees and into Parliament Square gardens where they began immediately to potter around in a perfectly pigeon-like way picking up crumbs and preening themselves. And at a casual glance you wouldn't have noticed that there was anything odd about them: pigeon-sized and pigeon-coloured, behaving like pigeons, surrounded by perfectly normal pigeons. How often do you look closely at a London pigeon, to check that it's exactly the same as the others?

The first person to pay any attention to them was an elderly Member of Parliament who had popped out for a breath of fresh air and was having a sit down on one of the benches. He looked at them and then quickly looked away again and wished he hadn't had that large and rich meal last night. He closed his eyes for a moment and promised himself he'd take things a bit more easily from now on and when he opened them again the gryphons were nowhere to be seen so he heaved a sigh of relief and hurried back into Parliament.

The gryphons, in fact, were now circling round an old lady who was feeding the birds with the end of a loaf. She stared at them and then got out her other glasses and stared harder. Then, being a sensible person, she went to fetch the nearest policeman.

The policeman strolled over. He was used to being told by dear little old ladies that something funny was going on. "Yes, madam," he said indulgently. "There," said the old lady, pointing. The gryphons were now busy pecking up the remains of a bag of crisps that they had found.

The policeman looked more closely. He swallowed, and cleared his throat. He blinked and looked again. "Like in *Alice in Wonderland*," said the old lady fondly. "Only smaller." Several people had now gathered;

95

there was a buzz of interested comment. The policeman began to talk crisply into his walkie-talkie; somebody tried to catch one of the gryphons, which moved off smartly and perched on some railings. "None of that," said the policeman. "Now then, everyone move along, please, there's nothing to look at." Everyone hung around. The tourists got out their cameras, and thus it was that a somewhat blurred enlargement of a photo of one of the gryphons (holding a bacon-flavoured crisp in its right front claw) appeared on the front page of the *Sun* the next morning.

In the meantime, though, the policeman had had a word with his superintendent and the superintendent had sent an inspector along to Parliament Square gardens and by the time the inspector had arrived the gryphons had disappeared. There were just pigeons: ordinary straightforward Westminster pigeons. If it hadn't been for the old lady and the other people who were still hanging around and only too pleased to swear the gryphons had been there—and of course that photo the next day—the policeman would have had a telling-off. As it was, the inspector decided to send a brief report of the matter to the people at the Zoo, and leave it at that.

The Curator of Birds at the Zoo saw the photo in the *Sun*, anyway, because one of the keepers brought it to him, for a joke. "Better get one of them, sir, hadn't we? Be a bigger draw than a baby panda." The Curator laughed, and agreed that it would. But then, half an hour later, he opened his mail and read the police inspector's report, and half an hour after that his secretary came in to say that three different people had telephoned to say that they had seen freak pigeons in Westminster. With little tails. And four legs. The Curator of Birds frowned and tapped his fingers on his desk and then he got up and pulled on his raincoat and went down to Parliament Square in a taxi.

A good half dozen or so of the gryphon chicks had left their nests by now. The first one that the Curator saw was perched on the arm of a bench preening a wing. An old man was sitting within three feet of it, reading a newspaper. He glanced at it once and returned to the newspaper. Well, he may have had bad sight.

The Curator closed his eyes for ten seconds. He felt quite dizzy. The last time he could remember feeling anything like this was when he opened a cage brought by a bird collector and found within it a kind of South American parrot that was considered to be more or less extinct. But this was worse: ten times worse. "No," he whispered. "It's impossible." He opened his eyes. The gryphon was still there. It turned its head and looked at him for a moment and then flapped over to a flower-bed.

The Curator rose to his feet, slowly and casually, and moved, even more slowly and casually, towards the gryphon. At that point he caught sight of another one, emerging from under a bush. He cursed himself for not having brought a camera. He slipped off his raincoat and moved very very gently towards the gryphon, which was unconcernedly pecking at an old sandwich, and prepared to drop the raincoat on top of it. At which point both gryphons took off smartly and flew up into the nearest tree.

The Curator decided to waste no more time. He went to the nearest telephone and called a very important policeman he knew and an even more important Cabinet Minister and within half an hour the whole of Parliament Square was cordoned off and the worst traffic jam that had ever been known had built up in central London. Some people said it was another of those demonstrations and others said knowingly there'd been a bomb thrown at the Prime Minister and large crowds gathered to gaze over the barriers into Parliament Square gardens where two dozen policemen and several people from the Zoo including the Curator were prowling around with cameras and things like enormous butterfly nets.

The gryphons sat in the top of a tall tree, or on the buttresses of the Abbey, and watched.

That was Day One. By Day Two it was on the evening television news and on Day Three every newspaper in the country was full of letters saying what ought or ought not to be done. The Royal Society for the Protection of Birds had a march to Downing

Street to hand in a petition demanding that the whole of the Embankment should be turned into a gryphon sanctuary and Parliament moved for the time being into Wembley Stadium (it was June, and good dry weather). The Save Britain's Heritage people wanted them declared a national monument immediately and the National Union of Farmers said they must be classified as dangerous pests and shot before they got out of hand. Meanwhile more gryphons came down from their nests. The Curator of Birds borrowed his son's scout tent and set up camp in Parliament Square gardens. The gryphons were counted and filmed. The Curator and the President of the Royal Society for the Protection of Birds were now having a furious row about whether or not a pair should be caught for the Zoo. The Curator insisted that it was absolutely essential in the interests of science; the President pointed out that there would be violent objections to this by bird-lovers. The Curator got in such a state that he began to argue that they could hardly be said to be birds anyway and then thought better of it, remembering that in that case his old enemy the Curator of Reptiles would probably get them.

On Day Six Parliament, which had been having a succession of emergency debates, passed the Gryphon Protection Act. No gryphon was to be killed, caught or otherwise molested, on pain of the most terrible penalties. A number of Members of Parliament had been in favour of bringing back hanging, or even beheading, but in the end they settled for fines of half a million pounds and life imprisonment.

By this time there were sixty or seventy gryphons. Some of them became more adventurous and were seen south of the river outside the National Theatre and wandering along the parapets of Waterloo Bridge. Zoologists from all over the world descended upon London and could be seen in droves, slung about with

cameras and causing yet more traffic jams. Every television station in the world wanted to send a film crew to make a film about gryphons; Parliament had to pass another act requiring written permission from the Queen for everyone wanting to do this. The Queen was asked to write as slowly as possible, or the whole situation would become unmanageable.

The pigeon parents watched it all with astonishment. They didn't know whether to be proud or ashamed. Since pigeons don't in any case have much to do with their offspring once they've left the nest they didn't feel any great attachment to the gryphons but a lot of the mothers continued to be distressed. They said they felt as though they'd been made use of in some way. The old pigeon—he who roosted on the head of Edward the Confessor—tried to console them: they'd go down in history, he said, as the parents of the most remarkable brood there'd ever been. The pigeon mothers didn't find this a great deal of help; they said they'd never wanted to be conspicuous, just to do their duty and bring up an ordinary clutch of chicks, as in any other year.

But in any case no one was paying much attention to the parents though there was a good deal of speculation about what could have caused it all. Scientists became interested in what the parent pigeons had been feeding on, and since this of course was mainly bits of people's sandwiches and buns and rolls there was a scare that it was something to do with that and a lot of anxious human mothers stopped giving bread to their children and several factories making it went out of business. Other people said darkly the government were behind it and a rather wild clergyman from Cornwall kept announcing that it was the beginning of the end of the world so the Archbishop of Canterbury had to step in and make a television announcement saying firmly that it wasn't but that it was all extremely interesting and we should be proud that we could still do things that other countries couldn't.

The President of the United States wrote a private letter to the Queen reminding her what good friends they were and what a special relationship they had and hinting that he'd like a really nice Christmas present this year. He and his wife just loved birds, he said, especially unusual kinds.

The Russian President sent a formal note to the Prime Minister offering two-thirds of Siberia in exchange for a pair of gryphons.

The Chinese offered six pandas for a pair.

The French suggested a straight swap for the Eiffel Tower.

The Japanese said they'd give a miniature portable television set, a pocket calculator and an electric train set to every child in the country if they could have a pair of gryphons. This was a cunning plan and caused a lot of trouble once it got out, resulting in another

march on Downing Street, this time by two thousand children from Birmingham who thought it was an interesting idea. But two thousand other children from Manchester didn't, and marched next day with banners declaring KEEP BRITISH GRYPHONS IN BRITAIN!

The numbers of tourists got quite out of hand. They arrived at Heathrow in plane loads, every day; all the hotels in London were booked out. They cruised around in buses labelled CENTRAL LONDON SAFARI TOURS and SPECIAL GRYPHON EXCURSION, pointing their cameras at anything in sight.

And of course not everyone behaved well. An unpleasant pet-shop proprietor from Penge caught one of the gryphons under the arches of Waterloo Bridge, on a dark evening, unseen by anyone, and sold it the next day for a sum of money that would astonish you to an equally unpleasant Spanish zoo-owner. The Spaniard tried to smuggle it out of the country in a Sainsbury's carrier bag, and would have got away with it had not a sharp-eared customs official at Heathrow heard scrabblings. There was the most terrible scene, during which the Spaniard had to be rescued by the police from a furious crowd. The gryphon was brought back to Westminster by the head of the Metropolitan Police and released. A special service of thanksgiving was held in the Abbey. The pet-shop proprietor is in Wormwood Scrubs to this day, I'm afraid.

Then there was the problem of the gryphons' diet. As you can imagine, they were being vastly overfed. Coachloads of tourists, hundreds of children, everyone plying them with crisps and crumbs and peanuts. They became extremely fat; some of them became so fat that they could hardly get airborne any more. Several were found staggering around in a bad way and had to be taken temporarily into the Zoo Sanatorium. Finally Parliament passed another Act making it illegal to feed the gryphons, and a special Gryphon Supply Van toured the area every day to see that the gryphons got enough food but not too much. Some people were already saying that they should all be rounded up and kept in an enormous aviary in Hyde Park for their own protection. Most people, though, felt even more strongly that a country that couldn't provide a decent way of life for free-range gryphons was in a poor way.

What everyone was waiting to see, of course, was what would happen when the next breeding season came round. Would there be hundreds more gryphons? Or none?

Gryphon fever raged all that summer. There was a special item at the end of the BBC news every day called The Gryphon Summary, reporting on how and where the gryphons were. All the newspapers carried plans of Westminster pinpointing where gryphons had been spotted the day before. Everyone was wearing gryphon T-shirts and singing the Gryphon Song and sticking up gryphon posters in their bedrooms. The school holidays ended and the days got shorter and cooler; it was autumn. Now pigeons, as you know, do not migrate; they are stay-at-home creatures like starlings and sparrows or like you and me and they stop here all the year round. It never occurred to anyone that the gryphons would not do the same. Imagine, then, the horror of those who understood bird behaviour when, one sunny October day, the gryphons all started to line up on the telephone wires high above Parliament Square, flapping their wings and chattering among themselves.

The Curator of Birds, pale and shaking, telephoned the Queen and the Prime Minister. "Is it normal for them to migrate?" asked the Queen. No one could answer this question. The Prime Minister rushed off to send telegrams to all other Prime Ministers everywhere making it clear that any migrating gryphons were British property and must be treated as such. The Curator of Birds sat on a bench and gazed mournfully at the gryphons, who combed their feathers with their claws, swished their snake-like tails and cocked their eagle-eyes at the gathering crowds beneath.

Word had got round. By the evening of that day there were huge silent throngs of people outside the Houses of Parliament, watching the gryphons. The band of the Scots Guards came, and played "Will ye no come back again?" a great many times. The BBC interrupted all programmes every fifteen minutes and when at last as dusk fell the whole flock of gryphons rose into the air, circled three times above Big Ben and then lifted higher and higher above the Thames the nation was able to watch their departure from its sitting-room. Lots of people were in tears, though no one could have said exactly why.

They never came back. Unlike swallows and other reliable birds who know the rules of migration. But then, they weren't ordinary birds, were they? They never came back and no gryphon has ever hatched again from any nest on Westminster Abbey or any other cathedral. Scientists have been trying to find explanations ever since, and people who are as old as I am still remember the summer of the gryphons and have our gryphon T-shirts tucked away somewhere in a drawer.

And where did they go? That's another mystery. Bird watchers have watched for them from Greenland to the Falkland Islands, without ever a glimpse. Perhaps no one will ever find out. Gryphons, remember, are an ancient race, far older than pigeons or humans; they know about things other creatures have forgotten. Maybe, in some remote mountain pass, or on the shores of some undiscovered lake, there is a flock of gryphons, peaceably living and breeding far from the tourists and the traffic. I rather hope so.

The Great Mushroom
Mistake

Birthday presents for mothers can be a problem. In the first place there is the expense. Obviously diamond necklaces and holidays in Bermuda are out of the question, even if your mother is the sort of person who would fancy such things. In the second place there is the difficult matter of choice. A present should be just what the person wants; to know what this might be you have to make a study of the person in question.

Sue and Alan Hancock had studied their mother as much as most children. That is to say, they knew warning signs of ill temper (a generally frowsty appearance, a tendency to say no in reply to any request) and signs of a good mood when almost anything might be allowed (humming while making the beds, preparation of large meals). And they could hardly help knowing what she was interested in.

Mrs Hancock was good at growing things. The Hancocks' garden did not just bloom: it crackled and exploded and positively burst out with leaf and petal. Mrs Hancock had green fingers, to put it simply. Everything she planted came popping out of the ground and then shot outwards and upwards; her roses and her peas were the envy of the neighbourhood. Whenever she had a spare minute she was out in the garden. Indeed when the children were small they had been vaguely under the impression that their mother could not stand up straight, because their most usual view of her was of someone bent double like a clothes-peg, peering down at her seedling plants, or scraping and scratching at the soil.

And so birthday presents were not really a problem. There were new trowels and new gardening gloves and special plants and hanks of new twine. But this year they wanted something special—something different, something no one else's mother had. They searched the usual shops, and were not satisfied. Indeed, it was not until the very day before the birthday that they walked past the greengrocer on the corner near their school and saw the very thing.

Outside the shop were two shallow wooden boxes from which bubbled a profusion of gleaming white mushrooms: crisp fresh delicious-looking mushrooms. And alongside the boxes was a notice: GROW YOUR OWN MUSHROOMS! A NEW CROP EVERY DAY!

They looked at each other. Their mother had grown just about everything in her time, but never mushrooms. They went into the shop. They bought a small plastic bag labelled MUSHROOM SPORE, another bag of earthy stuff in which you were supposed to plant it, and an instruction leaflet.

Mrs Hancock was thrilled. She couldn't wait to get going. The instruction leaflet said that the mushrooms liked to grow indoors in a darkish place. A cellar would do nicely, it said, or the cupboard under the stairs. The Hancocks had no cellar and the cupboard under the stairs was full of the sort of thing that takes refuge in cupboards under the stairs: old shoes and suitcases and a broken tennis racket and a chair with only three legs. Mrs Hancock decided that the only place was the cupboard in the spare room, which was used by guests only and no guest was threatening for some while. The children helped her to spread the earthy stuff out in boxes and scatter the spore. Then, apparently, all they had to do was wait.

During the night, Alan woke once and thought he heard a faint creaking sound, like a tree straining in the wind. And when, in the morning, they opened the door of the spare room cupboard there in the boxes was a fine growth of mushrooms—fat adult mushrooms and baby mushrooms pushing up under and around them. Mrs Hancock was delighted; the children preened themselves on the success of their present; everyone had fried mushrooms for breakfast.

The next day they found the cupboard door half open and mushrooms tumbling out onto the floor. "Gracious!" said Mrs Hancock. "It'll be mushroom soup for lunch today." The instruction leaflet said DO NOT SOW MORE SPORE TILL CROPPING CEASES, so they decided to wait and see what happened. The next day there were as many mushrooms again. They had mushrooms for every meal.

On the third day there were not only mushrooms bursting from the cupboard but a small clutch under the washbasin. There were far too many to eat; Mrs Hancock gave some to the postman and the milkman and the people next door.

That night, the creaking was more definite. Both children heard it; a sound something between a rustling and a splitting—the sound of growth. And in the morning there were mushrooms all over the spare room floor, a clump on the stairs and several clusters under the table in the hall. The Hancocks gazed at them

111

in astonishment. "They *are* doing well," said Mrs Hancock, with a slight trace of anxiety in her voice. It took some time to collect them all up, and the people next door said thanks very much but they couldn't really do with any more. The children were getting heartily tired of mushroom soup. In the end they had to throw a lot away.

Over the next few days, the mushroom invasion continued. They found mushrooms in the bathroom and beside the cooker and in the toy chest. When they

got up in the mornings they had to walk downstairs on a carpet of small mushrooms which squeaked faintly underfoot, like colonies of mice. It was when Mrs Hancock had to vacuum mushrooms from the sitting room carpet that they realised the situation had got quite out of control. "Stop planting the things," said Mr Hancock. "I have," wailed Mrs Hancock. "I only ever did plant them the once. They just keep coming." "Green fingers," said her husband sourly. "That's the trouble." Everyone looked despairingly at Mrs Hancock's hands: perfectly ordinary sensible-looking hands but clearly, in this instance, fatal.

They filled the dustbins with mushrooms. They took plastic sacks of mushrooms to the town dump. And still they came, bubbling up every night, springing cheerfully from window ledges and skirting-boards and behind pictures. The house smelled of mushroom: a clean, earthy smell.

Mrs Hancock called in the Pest Control Service, a business-like man with a van who took one look at the mushrooms and shook his head in perplexity. "I've never seen anything like it," he said. "Now if it was rats or cockroaches I'd know where I was. Or wasps. Or ants. This is phenomenal." He looked out of the window at the garden, and then at Mrs Hancock; "I'd say you had a way with nature, madam. Ever thought of going into the wholesale business?" He left a can of weedkiller and said he would come back in a few days. Mrs Hancock mopped the whole house out with weedkiller. The next morning, the night's growth of mushrooms looked a little sickly, like someone who has had a late night and a touch of indigestion, but the day after they were as thriving as ever, coming up here there and everywhere so that the floors of every room looked softly cobbled. The children were sent out to buy yet more black plastic sacks.

The Pest Control man shook his head again. "They've got a hold," he said. "That's what. Frankly, I don't know what to suggest. It's interesting, mind. I wouldn't let the papers get onto it—you could find yourself on the front page." The Hancocks stared at him coldly. "I'll have a think," he said, going out of the front door. "The great thing is, don't panic."

That evening, Mrs Hancock said, "There's nothing for it. We're going to have to call in Aunt Sadie." There was a silence; Mr Hancock sighed. "A desperate measure," he said. "But I see your point."

Many families have an Aunt Sadie: an expert all-purpose undefeatable long-distance interferer. The relation who scents defects as soon as she has one foot inside the door—"Pity that paint turned out the wrong colour," "I see Sue's hair's still growing dead straight," "I'm wondering if Alan's teeth don't need a brace." Aunt Sadie could kill any occasion stone dead: Christmas, birthdays, family outings. Strong men fled at the sight of Aunt Sadie. And there was nothing Aunt

Sadie enjoyed more than muscling in on a situation (preferably uninvited) and, as she called it, "lending a willing hand." What chance, Mr Hancock agreed, would a few mushrooms have against Aunt Sadie?

Aunt Sadie, dropping her suitcase in the hall, stalked through the house inspecting. She peered at the mushrooms and the mushrooms, just starting on their second crop of the day, peeped back from cracks in the floorboards and sidled out from under the carpets. She fetched the dustpan and shovelled out a couple of pounds of them from inside the grandfather clock, where they had been surging up unnoticed for several days. The Hancocks watched with interest. Aunt Sadie, in her time, had reduced a six foot traffic warden to tears and disrupted an entire police station. She went upstairs and could be heard tramping around. When she came down Mr Hancock said, "Well, Sadie—bit out of your line, eh?" This, of course, was meant to provoke, and it did.

Aunt Sadie glared at him. "I'll want a free hand. I'll want everyone out of the way except the children. You'd better take Mary for a short holiday."

"But I don't want a holiday . . ." Mrs Hancock began.

"You'll have to. There's no two ways about it. It's having you here that's encouraged the things. I always said all that gardening was unnatural." She rolled up her sleeves.

"What do you want *us* for?" asked Sue.

"Labour force," snapped Aunt Sadie.

The next few days were pandemonium. "There's nothing," said Aunt Sadie decisively, "that a good spring clean won't deal with." Carpets, curtains, chairs and tables were hurled hither and thither. The house looked as though a bomb had hit it. The children scurried to and fro with buckets and scrubbing-brushes.

The mushrooms grew, undaunted.

The children were sent shopping. "Ten gallons of disinfectant!" said the manager of the hardware shop. "Jeyes Fluid *and* ammonia *and* a quart of insecticide! You people in some kind of trouble?"

Aunt Sadie, with the children panting behind her, scrubbed and sprayed and swabbed. For five days she and the mushrooms did battle. A dose of Jeyes Fluid had them coming up blackened but valiantly fighting back. Insecticide and flea powder sent them reeling for a couple of days. "We've got them on the run!" said Aunt Sadie grimly, but then a new wave broke out from the airing cupboard. The war was on again.

All this had quite distracted Aunt Sadie from her usual occupation when visiting: general interference. In the normal way of things she would have been busy suggesting that everything the family did should be done differently and in particular that the children were a total disaster in terms of appearance, behaviour and anything else you like to mention. Their health, especially, was of intense interest: they were spotty, she would announce, or pasty-looking, or too large or too small or too fat or too thin, and various appalling tonics and potions were produced to set matters right.

With relief, Sue and Alan realised that on this occasion she was far too taken up with the mushrooms to pay them much attention at all. Until one evening Alan made the mistake of coughing.

"You've got a cough," said Aunt Sadie, instantly alert.

"Bit of biscuit got stuck," said Alan hastily.

"I know a chronic cough when I hear one," said Aunt Sadie, grim. She reached into the enormous handbag that accompanied her even into the bathroom. Out came a bottle of fearsome-looking brown stuff, and a spoon. "Open your mouth."

Whether what happened next was an accident or not will never be known. As the first horrific whiff of the cough mixture reached Alan's nose he gave a kind of convulsive snort. The cough mixture blew from the spoon, the spoon flew from Aunt Sadie's hand, Aunt Sadie with a cry of annoyance leaned forward to rescue it and knocked over the open bottle upon the table, which lurched to the floor gushing thick brown cough mixture in all directions. Everyone began to blame everyone else until suddenly Sue cried, "Look!"

The advancing tide of cough mixture had reached a clump of mushrooms that had sprung up unnoticed from the skirting-board. And as it did so a very curious thing happened. The mushrooms vanished. They simply expired. One moment they were there and the next there was nothing but a little heap of dust and a puddle of cough mixture.

"Well!" said Aunt Sadie, staring. "That's interesting . . ."

"If it does that to people too," said Alan, "it's a jolly good thing I didn't swallow it."

Aunt Sadie ignored him. "I think," she said thoughtfully, "we may be on to something."

This time Aunt Sadie did the shopping herself. It is not just anyone who can persuade a chemist to make up several gallons of cough mixture, and supply it in a large can with a spray attachment. What the chemist said or thought is not known; Aunt Sadie had a way of discouraging unwelcome curiosity. Anyway, she returned, armed with the new weapon, and set to work. And within a matter of hours there was not a mushroom in sight, nor did any appear the next morning, nor the next. Aunt Sadie stalked around the house in triumph, and sent for Mr and Mrs Hancock. The children, eyeing the remains of the cough mixture with awe, were quite extraordinarily careful not to cough.

And that was the end of the great mushroom mistake. For her next birthday the children gave their mother six handkerchiefs and some talcum powder, an unadventurous present but a safe one. And Aunt Sadie's reputation soared to even greater heights; there was nothing, it was generally agreed, with which she could not deal. The government, Mr Hancock suggested, would do well to hire her and keep her in hand for use in case of riots, epidemics, earthquake or flood. And the Pest Control man, who happened to call back the day before Aunt Sadie left, is still trying to get the recipe for that cough mixture from her.